W9-AMM-514

# BONES
## and the DINOSAUR Mystery

A Puffin Easy-to-Read

BY DAVID A. ADLER

ILLUSTRATED BY BARBARA JOHANSEN NEWMAN

PUFFIN BOOKS

For Michael and Deborah —D. A.

"For THE guys in my life: Phil, Dave, Mike, and Ben. Gotta love 'em!" —B. J. N.

PUFFIN BOOKS
Published by the Penguin Group
Penguin Young Readers Group, 345 Hudson Street, New York, New York 10014, U.S.A.
Penguin Group (Canada), 9 Eglinton Avenue East, Suite 700, Toronto, Ontario, Canada M4P 2Y3
(a division of Pearson Penguin Canada Inc.)
Penguin Books Ltd, 80 Strand, London WC2R 0RL, England
Penguin Ireland, 25 St Stephen's Green, Dublin 2, Ireland
(a division of Penguin Books Ltd)
Penguin Group (Australia), 250 Camberwell Road, Camberwell, Victoria 3124, Australia
(a division of Pearson Australia Group Pty Ltd)
Penguin Books India Pvt Ltd, 11 Community Centre, Panchsheel Park,
New Delhi – 110 017, India
Penguin Group (NZ), 67 Apollo Drive, Rosedale, North Shore 0632, New Zealand
(a division of Pearson New Zealand Ltd)
Penguin Books (South Africa) (Pty) Ltd, 24 Sturdee Avenue, Rosebank,
Johannesburg 2196, South Africa

Registered Offices: Penguin Books Ltd, 80 Strand, London WC2R 0RL, England

First published in the United States of America by Viking,
a division of Penguin Young Readers Group, 2005
Published by Puffin Books, a division of Penguin Young Reader Group, 2009

1 3 5 7 9 10 8 6 4 2

Text copyright © David A. Adler, 2005
Illustrations copyright © Barbara Johansen Newman, 2005
All rights reserved

THE LIBRARY OF CONGRESS HAS CATALOGED THE VIKING EDITION AS FOLLOWS:
Adler, David A.
Bones and the dinosaur mystery / written by David A. Adler ;
illustrated by Barbara Johansen Newman.
p. cm.
Summary: Young Detective Jeffrey Bones investigates the disappearance of the
plastic dinosaur his grandfather just bought for him in a museum gift shop.
ISBN 0-670-06010-0 (hardcover)
[1. Lost and found possessions—Fiction. 2. Museums—Fiction. 3. Grandfathers—Fiction.
4. Dinosaurs—Fiction. 5. Mystery and detective stories.]
I. Newman, Barbara Johansen, ill. II. Title.
PZ7.A2615Bof 2005—[Fic]—dc22 2004017392

Puffin Books ISBN 978-0-14-241341-8
Puffin and Easy-to-Read® are registered trademarks of Penguin Group (USA) Inc.

Manufactured in China

Except in the United States of America, this book is sold subject to the condition
that it shall not, by way of trade or otherwise, be lent, re-sold, hired out, or otherwise
circulated without the publisher's prior consent in any form of binding or cover
other than that in which it is published and without a similar condition
including this condition being imposed on the subsequent purchaser.

The publisher does not have any control over and does not assume
any responsibility for author or third-party Web sites or their content.

Reading level 2.2

# - CONTENTS -

# 1. Hello, Bones

"Hello, dinosaur bones.

I'm Bones, too.

I'm Detective Jeffrey Bones.

I solve mysteries."

"Hey," Grandpa called. "Look at this!"

I looked. It was a big dinosaur

with really big teeth.

I went to Grandpa and the dinosaur.

Sally was there, too.

She's Grandpa's friend.

"This is T-rex," Grandpa told me.

"When it was alive

it weighed five tons."

That's a lot of dinosaur.

I showed T-rex my detective bag.

"I've got great stuff in here," I said.

"Take a look at this."

I showed him my walkie-talkie set.

"I bet you never saw

one of these before," I said.

I walked around T-rex.

I read about him, too.

He was a meat eater.

Now that I can read,

I can find things out myself.

"Hey, Grandpa," I said

to the man standing next to me.

"Did you know T-rex

ate other dinosaurs?"

I looked up.

"Hey," I told the man.

"You're not my grandfather."

"I know that," the man said.

"Where is my grandfather?"

I asked the man.

"Where's Sally?"

"I don't know," the man said.

"I don't know either," I told him,

"but I'm a detective,

and detectives find things.

I'll find my grandfather

and Sally."

# 2. Little Blue T-Rex

It was easy for me

to find Grandpa and Sally.

They're old. They like to sit.

I just looked for a bench,

and there they were.

"Hey, Jeffrey," Sally said.

"Let's go to the gift shop.

We'll get a dinosaur

for you to take home."

"Oh, no," I told Sally.

"My parents say

I'm too young to have a pet."

Sally and Grandpa laughed.

"This won't be a real dinosaur,"

Grandpa said.

That's too bad, I thought.

I'd love to have a five-ton pet.

I followed the signs to the gift shop.

Grandpa and Sally followed me.

Sally picked up a large cloth dinosaur.

"I'm buying this for Michael," she said.

"He's my grandson."

Sally paid a man for it.

The man put the cloth dinosaur

in a large green bag.

Grandpa showed me a box

of small plastic dinosaurs.

"Pick one of these," he said.

I picked a blue T-rex.

Grandpa paid the man,

and he put my T-rex

in a small green bag.

I showed Sally my T-rex.

"That's so cute," Sally said.

She bought a pink plastic dinosaur

for her granddaughter Nancy.

It wasn't a T-rex.

She paid for it,

and it was put in a green bag, too.

Then she bought a dinosaur puppet

and a dinosaur oven mitt.

"I'll use this mitt when I cook," Sally said.

"Cook!" Grandpa said.

"Did you say 'cook'?

You know cooking makes me hungry."

Then Grandpa looked at me and asked,

"Aren't you hungry?"

"Yes and no," I said.

"I'm not hungry for vegetables,

but I am hungry for ice cream."

"Then we'll get ice cream," Grandpa said.

We went to the snack place.

I got a dish of strawberry ice cream.

Grandpa and Sally got cups of tea

and a piece of coffee cake to share.

The snack place was crowded,

but we found a table.

I put my green bag on the table

and ate my ice cream.

Sally put her green bags on the table.

When we were all done

with the tea, cake, and ice cream

Grandpa said, "Let's go and see

the moon rocks."

There were pictures of the moon

and pictures taken on the moon.

There were moon rocks, too,

and a gift shop with toy moon rocks.

"Would you like a toy moon rock?"

Grandpa asked.

"No, thank you," I said.

"I have T-rex."

But I didn't!

"Hey," I said.

"Where's my green bag?

Where's my T-rex?"

# 3. Walkie-Talkie Time

"Maybe I left my T-rex

in the snack bar.

Maybe it's still on the table," I said.

Sally said, "My dinosaurs are right here."

She held up a large green bag.

I was happy for Sally and her grandchildren,

but I wasn't happy for me.

I wanted my blue plastic T-rex.

We went back to the snack place.

I looked at our table.

A boy and his father

were sitting there.

On the table there was ice cream

and juice, but no small green bag.

Grandpa, Sally, and I

went to the woman who sold snacks.

"Did anyone find a blue plastic T-rex

in a small green bag?" I asked.

"No," she said.

Hm, I thought.

I've got to do some detective work.

I opened my detective bag

and took out my walkie-talkies.

I gave one to Grandpa and one to Sally.

"Grandpa and I will go this way," I said.

I pointed to the tables by the windows

so Grandpa and Sally would know

which way was "this way."

"Sally, you can go the other way."

I pointed to the tables by the door.

"Please, look for my small green bag,"

I told Sally. "If you find it,

call me and Grandpa on the walkie-talkie."

Grandpa and I looked at the tables

near the window.

"Look at all these people," Grandpa said.

"People sure do get hungry

when they look at dinosaur bones."

"Hey!" I told Grandpa.

"Look over there."

A girl and her mother

were sitting at a table by the window.

On the table were salads,

cups of milk, and a small green bag.

I pushed the TALK button

on my walkie-talkie.

"Hey," I told Sally.

"I found T-rex."

Then I pointed at the small green bag.

"Hey," I said to the girl,

"what's in the bag?"

# 4. I Wanted T-Rex

"Oh, my," Grandpa said.

"First say hello."

So that's what I did.

"Hello," I said to the girl.

"What's in the bag?"

"It's a dinosaur," the girl said.

"I know it is," I told her.

"It's a blue plastic T-rex."

"Oh, no," she said.

"T-rex was a mean dinosaur.

T-rex was a meat eater.

I bought a plant eater."

She opened the bag

and showed me a plant eater.

I looked at the salads

the girl and her mother were eating

and knew why she wanted

a plant-eating dinosaur.

This girl and her mother

were plant eaters, too.

"Thank you," I said to the girl.

I looked up,

and there was Sally.

"This is silly," Sally said.

"We don't have to look and look

for your toy dinosaur.

We can just buy you another one."

Sally gave me my walkie-talkie.

I put the two walkie-talkies

in my detective bag.

I was happy I would get a new T-rex,

but I wasn't happy

about losing the old one.

I'm a detective.

Smart detectives find things.

Maybe, I thought,

I'm not such a smart detective!

We went to the gift shop.

I looked at all the small plastic dinosaurs.

There were lots of plant eaters,

but no T-rex dinosaurs.

I told the gift shop man,

"I want a blue T-rex."

"I'm sorry," he said.

"A small boy bought the last T-rex."

Then he looked at me.

"You're the boy who bought it."

Hey! I'm not small! I thought.

Grandpa said, "I'll buy you a different dinosaur."

But I didn't want a different dinosaur.

I wanted a T-rex.

# 5. I Am a Great Detective!

Grandpa, Sally, and I

left the gift shop.

We looked at pictures

taken from outer space.

We looked at pictures of Earth

and other planets.

We looked at pictures of animals

that are disappearing.

One day soon there may be no more

whooping cranes, gray wolves,

key deer, or California condors.

That reminded me of T-rex.

There are no more T-rex dinosaurs.

Next we saw how big animals

eat small animals.

I looked at the painting of a large fish

about to eat a smaller fish

that was about to eat an even smaller fish.

Then I looked at Sally.

Sally had a large green bag.

I smiled.

Maybe I am a good detective, I thought.

Maybe I solved the mystery

of my missing T-rex.

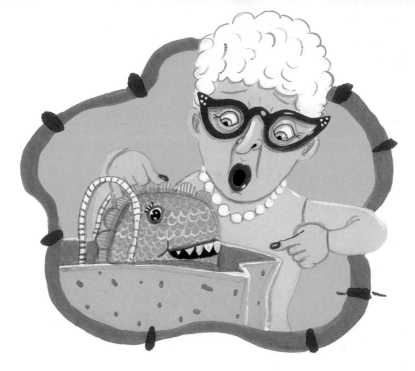

"Hey," I asked Sally.

"Where are all your small green bags?"

"In here," Sally said.

"I put the smaller bags in the big one."

Just like big fish

that eat smaller fish, I thought.

"Maybe you put my small green bag

in there, too," I said.

"Oh, my," Sally said.

"Maybe I did."

Sally sat on a bench

and opened the bag.

She took out the large cloth dinosaur

and put it on the bench.

Then she took out

four small green bags.

In one was a pink plastic dinosaur.

In the others were a dinosaur puppet,

a dinosaur oven mitt,

and my blue plastic T-rex.

I hugged my T-rex.

"I missed you," I said.

"So much has happened

since you disappeared."

"I'm sorry," Sally said.

"When I saw all these green bags

on the snack bar table,

I was afraid one would get lost."

"Well," I told Sally,

"I'm not sorry

you put my bag in yours.

You helped me prove

that I'm still a great detective."

31

Then I asked T-rex,

"You're lots of years old.

Have you ever met a better detective

than the great Jeffrey Bones?"

T-rex didn't answer.

I guess he never met

a better detective than me.